GW00363615

# ANDREW LLOYD W
# SHOWSTOPPERS
## Playalong *for* Alto Saxophone

**Wise Publications**
part of The Music Sales Group
London/New York/Paris/Sydney/Copenhagen/Berlin/Madrid/Tokyo

Published by
**Wise Publications**
8/9 Frith Street, London W1D 3JB, England.

Exclusive Distributors:
**Music Sales Limited**
Distribution Centre, Newmarket Road, Bury St. Edmunds,
Suffolk IP33 3YB England.
**Music Sales Pty Limited**
120 Rothschild Avenue, Rosebery, NSW 2018, Australia.

Order No. AM91936
ISBN 0-7119-4052-5
This book © Copyright 2005 by Wise Publications.

Compiled by Nick Crispin.
Edited by Christopher Hussey and Rebecca Taylor.
Music arranged by Quentin Thomas.
Music processed by Camden Music.
Cover photography by George Taylor.
Printed in Great Britain.

CD recorded, mixed and mastered by Jonas Persson and John Rose.
Alto Saxophone played by John Whelan.
Backing tracks:
'As If We Never Said Goodbye', 'Love Changes Everything', 'The Phantom Of The Opera',
'Superstar' and 'Whistle Down The Wind' arranged by Danny G.
'Close Every Door' and 'Pie Jesu' arranged by John Maul.
'Don't Cry For Me Argentina' and 'Memory' arranged by Paul Honey.
'Unexpected Song' arranged by Jeff Leach.

# Saxophone Fingering Chart

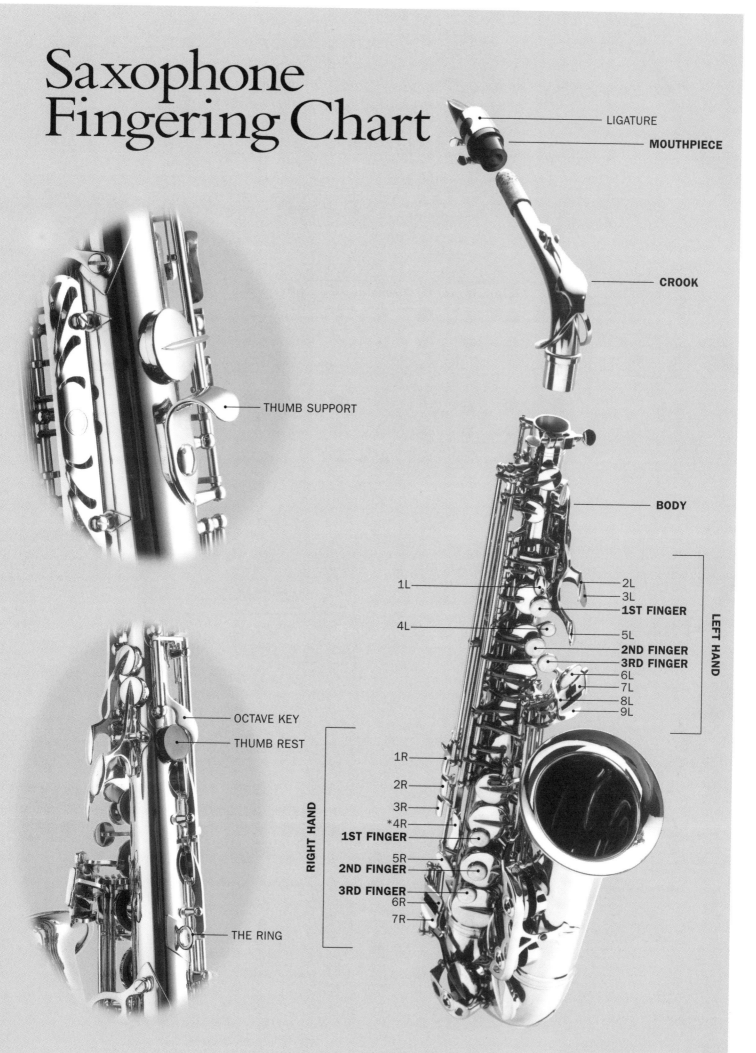

LIGATURE

**MOUTHPIECE**

**CROOK**

THUMB SUPPORT

**BODY**

1L — 2L
— 3L
— **1ST FINGER**
4L — 5L
— **2ND FINGER**
— **3RD FINGER**
— 6L
— 7L
— 8L
— 9L

**LEFT HAND**

OCTAVE KEY

THUMB REST

**RIGHT HAND**

1R
2R
3R
*4R
**1ST FINGER**
5R
**2ND FINGER**
**3RD FINGER**
6R
7R

THE RING

* Not fitted on some saxophones

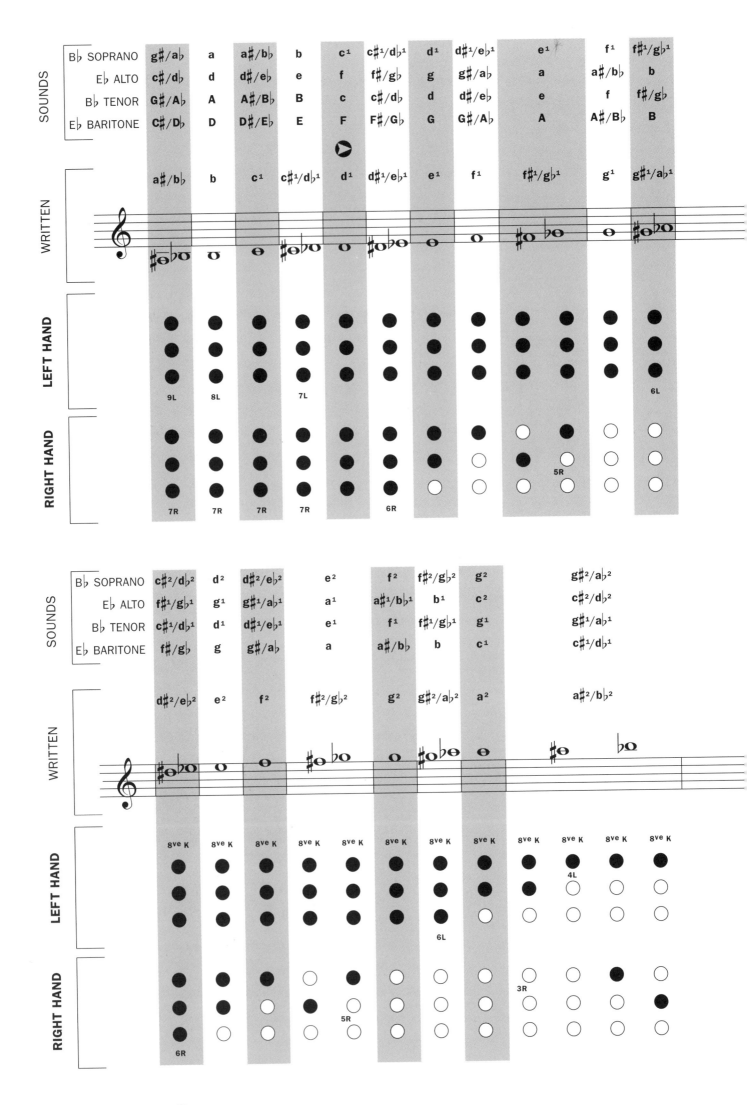

Indicates the lower limit of the best playing range

Indicates the upper limit of the best playing range

# As If We Never Said Goodbye

Music by Andrew Lloyd Webber
Words by Don Black & Christopher Hampton

**Moderato**

rit.

a tempo          piu mosso

molto allargando                    a tempo

# Close Every Door

Music by Andrew Lloyd Webber
Words by Tim Rice

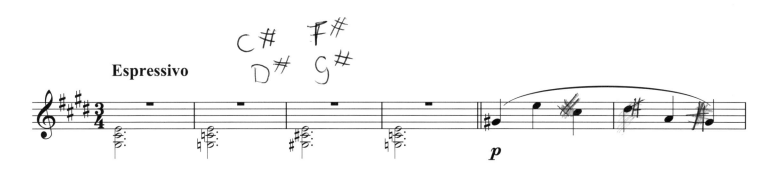

a tempo

rall.                                                   a tempo

molto rall.

# Love Changes Everything

Music by Andrew Lloyd Webber
Words by Don Black & Charles Hart

# Memory

Music by Andrew Lloyd Webber
Words by Trevor Nunn after T.S.Eliot

# The Phantom Of The Opera

Music by Andrew Lloyd Webber
Words by Charles Hart

**Allegro vivace**

**Fade to the end**

# Pie Jesu

**Music by Andrew Lloyd Webber**

# Don't Cry For Me Argentina

Music by Andrew Lloyd Webber
Words by Tim Rice

**Slowly**          **Tempo 1°**

**Slow tango feel**

poco rall.    Slower

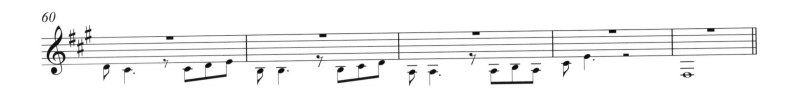

**Tempo 1º**

*mf*

*mp*

**Slower and freely**

*p*

rit.          **Refrain grandioso**

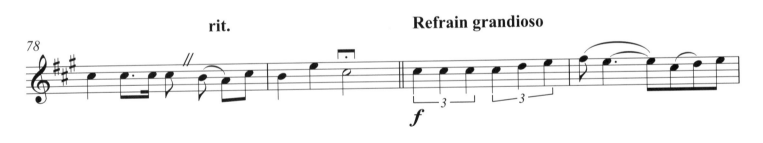

*f*

molto allargando      a tempo

*mp*

# Superstar

Music by Andrew Lloyd Webber
Words by Tim Rice

**Repeat 2 times and fade towards end**

# Unexpected Song

Music by Andrew Lloyd Webber
Words by Don Black

**rall.** **slower**

**rit.**

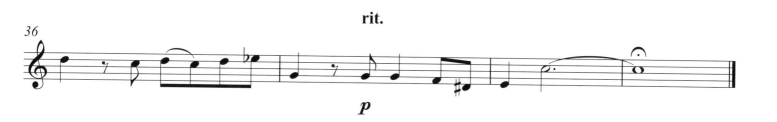

# Whistle Down The Wind

Music by Andrew Lloyd Webber
Words by Jim Steinman

**Moderato con moto**

molto allargando

a tempo, broadly

rall.